PACO DONG & THE DUCK DRAGON

PACO DONG & THE DUCK DRAGON

DAVID SLOCUM

Contents

1

Chapter 1.

Paco Dong and The Duck-Dragon: A Murder is Brewing.

Once upon a time, the Rio Grande was filled with folklore, like the weeping woman or dragon-alligators haunting people in the night, and now it is creating legends from myths in the border-lands.

Canutillo is a small town made from a three-mile triangle in the upper valley on the far west side of El Paso, Texas—the crossroads to the borderlands. South of the Rio is Mexico; just a mile west is New Mexico.

On this day, under the warming morning sun, a teenaged boy named Paco Dong walks down the riverbank of the Rio Grande, by the railroad tracks that ran, at this point, behind the Sun Brewing Motel.

In this crossroads on the riverbanks, in a muddy spot in a patch of tall grass, Paco chances upon a large trio of eggs. Paco stares at the eggs in amazement because they are like no eggs he has ever seen. They are roughly six inches in size, with some kind of goo around them. They are dark green in color with golden spots. They aren't thin bird eggs, like a chicken's; they are thick, and Paco cannot fathom where they could have come from.

Then, one of the eggs slowly hatches, and behold, a new creature never yet observed by mankind emerges.

This is no ordinary new species: It has a golden duck bill and shiny golden feathers with a green ring around its neck. At about the midsection, the feathers turn to a dark green and continue on down to a scaly tail not unlike a dragon's. The wings are half golden, half green, as are the legs and feet. The feet look like webbed talons and appear capable of grabbing and tearing as much as swimming.

Maybe the shallow river water of the Rio Grande holds the keys to the origin of life, Paco thinks. The Rio Grande has always had local ghost stories, mystical and spiritual folklore surrounding it here in the borderlands. From the Cucuy to the river of trapped souls clawing their way out onto the riverbanks in purgatory, cleansing their sins and trying to escape to the paradise city. There were even tall tales of miniature dragons and alligators no bigger than your hand swimming in the Rio Grande. The river has always had a mystical and magical quality about it.

This time, the egg came first! Paco is too young to understand the full mystery, how the spirits of the Rio Grande took the carbonate- and mineral-rich water and the mud teeming with organisms and synthesized the building blocks of life. He only knows he has been present for a miracle, the origin of a new lifeform.

A *pata-dragón*, he thinks. A duck-dragon.

Paco stares in bewilderment at the duck-dragon and kneels down to pick it up. The duck-dragon stares back at Paco, taking it all in and processing everything. Paco smiles and starts walking home with his new friend. Paco keeps the duck-dragon in an old Amazon box, out of the public eye, for fear someone will want to take it away from him. Paco plays with the duck-dragon and talks to it every day, and soon he thinks of it as his best friend. He names him Hoppy after his love for hoppy beer styles.

Paco, a high school dropout, started home-brewing when he was fifteen, inspired by the opening of the Sun Brewing Motel down the road when he was little. His father doesn't like the illegal activity, but he saw how it kept him out of trouble. His only goals in life are to be a beer truck driver and to keep his girlfriend. For Paco, being a beer truck driver would be the coolest thing ever. He lives alone in his father's single-story duplex apartment complex because his father is divorced and travels a lot. This allows Paco to develop his passions for brewing and for Mexican Taekwondo. It's evolved over the years to incorporate Mexican aggressive style boxing and the theatrical high-flying kicks of Korean Martial

Arts. This evolving martial art has been passed down from generation to generation. Paco's father taught him, as did his father before him.

As the years go by, Hoppy reveals he is preternaturally intelligent. He learns how to talk, read, and write in several languages. By human standards, Hoppy is a genius and has developed into his own creature with his own opinions and sense of humor. Hoppy did it mostly by reading, YouTube videos, and TV. Of course, Paco has a tremendous influence on the upbringing of Hoppy as well. Paco plays chess a lot with Hoppy and often talks chess history. Hoppy is a genius, but Paco is gifted at chess and is almost an idiot savant. Paco does have more talents and capabilities, it's just hard to see from the surface.

Paco and his father are Mexican immigrants to America from Torreon, Mexico. Paco's father, Wang Dong, is a Mexican of Korean descent. That makes Paco a Korean Mexican American. The Dong Family story, passed down from generation to generation, is that the original Dongs were smuggled into southern Mexico to be laborers for building infrastructure like railroads and highways. Wang always reminds Paco how his family worked very hard for the privileges they have today and that they live off of the backs of their ancestors.

Wang has always been very hard on Paco and views him as a disappointment. Wang is very proud of his other son, Ming, who was on scholarship to Harvard and is studying law. Paco and Ming couldn't be more opposite; Paco is a free spirit and doesn't take life too seriously, always laughing with a huge toothy smile, while Ming is the stoic, model son. Even Paco's girlfriend, Saavedra, is starting to struggle with her relationship with Paco. She's also the only person who knows of Paco's best friend Hoppy.

Paco and his father do have one major characteristic in common: They're both ladies' men. When Paco was born, his father was so proud of him, he held him up and said to everyone, look at my boy, my son, and he has a big pee pee! It's the one area where Paco is clearly better than Ming. Maybe Ming's penis envy gave him a major chip on his shoulder and inspired him to accomplish great things, while Paco got the winning personality, charisma, and sense of humor.

Saavedra is madly in love with Paco, who is tall, dark, and handsome with distinct Asian eyes, but even she has her limits. Her family is extremely wealthy and lives in a Mediterranean-style mansion on top of the mountain in the old west side of El Paso. Saavedra's parents, especially her father, always wanted Saavedra to end up with an educated man of high social status and a well-paying job, someone who could take care of her. Instead, she's with Paco, but they are in puppy love.

2

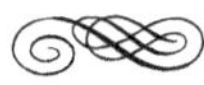

Chapter 2.

Saavedra walks into the living room area of Paco's apartment after getting cleaned up in the bathroom. She had a long day of work and is settling in for the evening. She sees Paco and Hoppy watching the MTV series *Beavis and Butthead* again while drinking beers and laughing. She huffs and stomps her foot and yells, Paco, I thought I told you if you don't stop watching *Beavis and Butthead* then I'm going to break up with you? Paco looks at Saavedra and laughs like Butthead: Huh huh huh... Huh huh... then Hoppy says, Do you have any T.P. for my bunghole so it doesn't get polio! Saavedra grimaces and says, You need to get a job! to which Paco responds, My dream job is to be a beer truck driver, and I'm working on it. Saavedra retorts, That's all the ambition you have, Paco! Paco affirms this: Yes, absolutely. That's my ambition in life and what I want to be. It's a noble job. Hoppy interjects by saying, In 1801, Guinness would go on sea voyages from Ireland to the West Indies, a.k.a. the Caribbean, to deliver porter beer, and the English would ship Russian Imperial Stouts to the Balkans and of course Russia. Beer delivery is indeed a noble profession.

Saavedra says, Good luck getting a job like that sitting on the couch, grabs her things, and announces she's leaving as she heads out the door to go home. Hoppy is a bit concerned, Bro, she's getting serious. Maybe you should walk over to the Sun Brewing Motel and ask Billy Bob for a job—brewing or delivering beer or something. You're always talking about how you've known Billy Bob since you were in elementary school. All your funny stories walking down the Rio Grande behind the brewery to go to school or coming back home. Paco responds, Yeah, you're right. Let's finish up this episode, then I'll head out and bring us back the bare essentials: Sun Brewing Lager and Aye Wey Burgers.

Paco walks to the Sun Brewing Motel and sits at the bar chatting with Chino, the bartender, asking him if he thinks Billy Bob would hire him. Ruben "Chino" Aragon is one of the original crew members from decades ago. Chino is also one of Billy Bob's closest friends and confidants. Chino and Billy Bob go way back and are both bikers. Chino has a long black and gray beard and is getting older, but everyone in the neighborhood loves Chino, and whatever he says pulls a lot of weight. Paco asks Chino, Say, are you a Chinese Mexican? Chino responds, No, but why do you ask? Paco responds, Because your name is Chino, and I've always wanted to ask you that but never have. Chino tells Paco, I'm born and raised right down the road here off the Rio Grande, I'm a Canuto. I'm Chicano, and as far as I know I have no Asian in me, but who knows? I might, people call me Chino because of my eyes. I don't have round eyes, and when I smile or laugh I look like a Mexican Mr. Miyagi. I'm actually a Korean Mexican, Paco explains. I'm a first generation Korean Mexican American. Chino responds, We provide a living wage here at The Sun Brewing Motel, none of that under-the-table stuff here where you work all day and night and get paid crap. Let me go talk to Billy Bob.

In only a few minutes, Chino returns with a smile on his face and tells Paco, Be here tomorrow at 6 a.m. and report to the lead brewer, Rupprecht. Thank you so much! Paco says. You're welcome. Billy Bob knows you and knows you're a brewer. You're going to start out an assistant brewer. That's great! I really appreciate it. Chino, put in an order to-go for me please: two Aye Wey burgers, two Big Kahuna Burgers, two Spam burgers, and a 12-pack of lager.

Paco arrives back home with the munchies and tells Hoppy the good news, how he just landed his first beer job. Hoppy congratulates him and says, Now, you better call Saavedra and let her know, too. Go call her, before she breaks up with you and finds someone else. She's a very attractive lady.

Paco calls Saavedra to tell her about his new job. She congratulates him, but Paco can hear she's still not so happy. Saavedra is a very attractive and bright woman who graduated from high school and college at the same time. She graduated top in her class and is already a nurse working in a hospital. She also goes to night school to continue her education. A lot of people in her family and at her work question her judgement in dating Paco. But Saavedra is under Paco's spell. She tells them all how not too many other people see how great he is because of his lack of social status. Saavedra sees a lot of potential in Paco; she's truly in love with him. She takes the good with the not so good, but at the same time, she believes in Paco when nobody else really does.

Just don't count your chicks just yet, she warns him. You've never had a job like this before. I know you can do it; I just hope you're being realistic about what it's going to take.

Paco ignores her and says, Let's to go out on a date night to celebrate! She asks him where he would like to go. For Paco, that was an easy question. He said, The Sun Brewing Motel! We can get a room and take their famous beer bath and order room service. Saavedra is suddenly concerned. I don't know. You've heard the rumors that that place is haunted. And people are still talking about that unsolved murder that is still being investigated over there. I'm happy you got the job you wanted, but let's go somewhere else. Paco responds, Okay, since you're paying, you can pick out the place we are going. Let's go to Elemi Mexican Restaurant, it's my favorite. Paco says, Oh that's right, the owner and chef was just in the news for being a James Beard award finalist. I love a chef's take on traditional Mexican food. My dad taught me how to make the family's chamoy sauce and kombucha that was passed down from generation to generation. I've always loved to cook myself and appreciate good food. I know, she assures him. I remember you telling me all about your family recipes. Your dad was telling me how chamoy sauce and the kombucha fermented beverage originated in China and all the ways Asian food helped shape Mexican cuisine. Paco responds, Yeah, I've got mongoloid blood. Hoppy chimes in, Uh, bro, you mean Mongol. *Mongoloid* is a racist term we don't use anymore. I mean whatever Genghis Khan was! Ah I see, says Hoppy. Of course, the concept of race has been disproven by genetics; you are all the same species. But I get what you mean. You mean a way of grouping people in a geographical location, like being Mexican, if you're from the same country or Latino if you're from anywhere south of the United States. It's exhausting talking to you sometimes, Hoppy. I know, and that's why I try to talk more in your species' language and dumb things down to short sentences or memes. Saavedra speaks up from the other end of the call: Are you done with your side bar conversation with Hoppy? Oh, sorry bonita. I'll wait for you to come pick me up.

Paco and Saavedra go out for a wonderful night. First, they eat a delicious dinner with a spectacular presentation of house made blue corn tortilla carnitas at Elemi, then they drive down the scenic route of El Paso and star gaze on top of the mountain while overlooking the cities of El Paso/Juarez. The only thing that separates the cities geographically is the Rio Grande, which is the border of not only the two cities but the two countries in this area.

They make it back to Paco's place and see Hoppy watching *Howard the Duck* while drinking beer. Hoppy looks at Paco and Saavedra as they walk through the front door towards him and says, You two love birds come watch this movie with me. Saavedra responds, We need to get ready for bed. We both have work tomorrow morning. Paco tells Hoppy, I see a pattern with you Hoppy, you seem to always be watching a movie related to ducks or dragons. Hoppy cries, Fire-breathing flying-V formation now! Paco responds, Right on! The quack attack, buddy! Come have a beer with me, Paco. Sure thang, buddy.

Saavedra tells Hoppy you need a girlfriend. Hoppy responds, I wish. It does get a bit lonely. Saavedra asks, Why do you think you're the only one of your kind? How is it possible you're the only duck-dragon ever in existence? Hoppy responds, It's because life willed it to be so. The building blocks of life came together at the perfect moment and willed me into existence. The egg really did come first, and I cracked out of the egg and became like all the other living organisms on earth.

Saavedra is speechless and tells them, Paco you stay and drink beer with Hoppy. I'm going home. Wait Saavedra, Me and Hoppy were discussing a while back why nobody has ever met a Mexican Dong before. Saavedra responds, That's an interesting question, Paco, but I'm leaving. Please please please stay, Saavedra? It's my family folklore. Okay, I'll stay, but only for a little while. Hoppy takes a big gulp of beer then looks at Saavedra and says, Excellente! Let me get you caught up: Paco was explaining that his father told him that you've had over a million Asian immigrants come to present-day Mexico since the days of New Spain. They were laborers building infrastructure, like roads, bridges, and railroads. So if all these Asian folks were living here, naturally the question came about, why does nobody know of any Asian names in Mexico, except in rare occurrences, like the Dong family? Paco explained that his dad told him back in them days, especially in the 15 and 1600s, there was a lot of slaves in New Spain, and most Asians had no immigration papers or identification. Consequently, the names changed over time, for example, Pong to Paco, Yang to Yanez, Ming to Montes, and so on and so forth.

Hoppy continues his synopsis: From historical records, even up to the 20th century, being assimilated was extremely important, and to avoid prejudice, Asians assimilated to become more Mexican. This would be a natural thing to do, to be a part of national pride. Today, you'll see a reclaiming of heritage, though. There are even small Chinatowns in Mexico nowadays. Saavedra chimes in and says, This has been an interesting history lesson. I look like a white girl—it's probably my Galician and Portuguese background. Paco belches then remarks, Yes, you're a white Mexican, and you're my little conquistadora, but it wouldn't surprise me if you had some Asian in you, too. I'll buy you a DNA test for your birthday. You do that, but I'm leaving now. You both keep drinking and belching like bullfrogs. I hate your beer breath, Paco.

Paco responds, Give me a kissy-kiss, Saavedra, and be proud of my mating calls. I finally got my dream job! I thought your dream job was to be a beer truck driver? That's true, but as a brewer, I'm learning chemistry and science. And guess what? I'll get to deliver my own beer.

Congratulations, Paco, I'm happy for you.

Chapter 3.

Paco arrives on time to work the next morning at the Sun Brewing Motel and meets with Billy Bob. Billy Bob gives him a tour of the brewery, restaurant, and motel, meeting everyone who works there along the way. Billy Bob takes Paco to introduce him to Rupprecht, Billy Bob's lead brewer. Paco meets Rupprecht but is a little surprised because Rupprecht has a slight German accent. Billy Bob explains to Paco that Rupprecht is a Bavarian-trained brewer from the Old World and is Afro-German. Rupprecht goes on to tell Paco his family emigrated from Germany to the borderlands because his father was an automation engineer who started his own company here with several government contracts. Paco asks Rupprecht, Who's the girl over there? Rupprecht responds, That's my sister, Bertha. She doesn't work here, but sometimes she comes to visit me and bring me good German food. Nothing like a nice Frankfurter, right Bertha? Bertha gives a wry smile. Right, says Rupprecht, She loves the wiennies. Paco says, Can I ask your full name, Bertha? She tells him, Bertha Bierhals Von Wallenrodt. That's a nice name, Bertha. Bertha asks him back, What's your full name, Pacochen? Paco Kong Dong, if you must know, he says, flashing her a huge smile. She shows him a lot of teeth in return. Billy Bob looks to the sky with his hands out and asks, Why me, Lord? You make men out of clay, but my men are made out of kaka! Billy Bob then tells Paco, I want you to shadow Rupprecht for the next two hours, but then I want you to go home and get some rest. Come back tonight at 10 p.m. You're working the graveyard shift because I need all these tanks cleaned by first shift tomorrow. You'll meet the other assistant brewer, Jon, who'll show you how it's done.

Paco goes home and tells Hoppy about his day over a morning beer. You'll never believe this Hoppy: I met some Germans today, and one of them is an expert Bavarian-trained brewer. The other one was his sister. They have long names and are Afro-Germans. Hoppy asks, What's the chicks name? Bertha Bierhals Von Wallenrodt. Hoppy has his unique laugh and tells Paco that is funny dude, her name means "famous beer neck." They must come from a long line of German brewers.

Paco asks Hoppy to come visit him at the brewery tonight, explaining he'll probably be working alone for much of the time. If the coast is clear, Hoppy, then fly or swim down to the brewery so I can show it to you, but wait for me to call. Sounds like a plan, amigo. Paco says, I'm going to finish this bowl of rice, chug this beer, then go mimis. Sweet dreams, friend.

Paco arrives for the graveyard shift, and Jon teaches him how to properly clean the tanks. Jon explains the basics of the brewery and how all the tanks are labeled. See these tanks over here, Paco? These tanks are in secondary fermentation, and see these tanks over here? These tanks are in primary fermentation. Leave all them tanks in fermentation alone. Don't touch them. You can see how they are all labeled. The tanks you'll need to worry about are all over here—see the labels? They say *fermentation complete* with a final gravity reading and *racked to keg* or *canned on* a certain date. I'll be back tomorrow morning to inspect everything. If you need anything or have any questions, then give me a call.

A few hours after Jon leaves, after he's cleaned most of the tanks, Paco calls Hoppy and tells him to fly over. Hoppy swims instead because it's less noticeable. The brewery sits on the riverbank, so it's easy for people to go in and out from the back without being noticed, especially at night. Paco lets Hoppy in through a backdoor around the corner from the back patio. Hoppy absolutely loves the brewery and is excited, and he has also been drinking all night. Hoppy tells Paco, Hey buddy, I've brought a 12-pack of your homebrew. We can chug a few beers while I'm here. Good forward thinking, Hoppy. That's what I love about you: You're always several steps ahead. Paco and Hoppy crack open some cans of beer and start discussing random subjects such as the beer and brewing Goddess Ninkasi.

Hoppy wanders around exploring and finds a tank that labeled "Meados de Alien Hazy Pale Ale." Hoppy tells Paco, I've got to open this tank up and take a look. Paco says, Okay. They both climb the ladder and open up the tank, and behold, they see something divine. The bubblies and yeast working their magic. Hoppy tells Paco, Please let me jump in there! It's my life's dream to swim in a beer tank filled with hoppy brew. Paco responds, You know you'll ruin that entire batch of beer if you do that Hoppy. Hoppy says, Just this once! Please don't deprive me of this! It's been my lifelong dream. Paco responds, Okay, do it; it's for a noble cause.

Hoppy jumps in the fermentation tank and immediately starts to lap up the newly forming beer as he swims around. Paco leans back against the railing and continues to drink his beer. This duck-dragon has an amazing ability to drink beer.

After a couple of hours, the beer in the tank is well over half way ingested. Hoppy keeps on with his quacking beer belches and continues sticking his head in the beer, taking big gulps. He sticks his head out of the tanks and lets out a thunderous and scary prolonged beer belch, then tells Paco to get in the tank with him. Paco has had one too many beers himself and only thinks to ask, Is it hot? It's warm for beer, but not for a person, Hoppy explains. Okay, says Paco. It's a once in a lifetime opportunity. Right, buddy! I'll need to clean this tank anyways. So Paco jumps in the tank and starts drinking beer with Hoppy too. They're both playing around, joking around, and drinking as much beer as they can. Another hour goes by and Hoppy finishes the entire tank of beer and they both curl up and lay down in the tank. They're both so full of the liquid they can barely move. At last Paco tells Hoppy, You need to get going, it's almost time for first shift to arrive.

Hoppy flies home while Paco stays in the tank trying not to move. He's never drunk so much beer in his life. Billy Bob shows up to the brewery a little later with Rupprecht. Billy Bob yells, Where the heck are you, Paco? Paco climbs out of the tank and farts incredibly loud. Then he continues to pass gas from all the ingestion of CO_2 in the beer. He's embarrassed, but there's nothing he can do.

Billy Bob yells again, Stop farting in my brewery! Then Billy Bob realizes something is very wrong with this picture. He asks Rupprecht, Why is Paco climbing out of the Meados de Alien Ale tank? Paco's rear end is exploring the entire range of farts, PFFT... FRAAAAAP... BR-RRRRRRRRRRT... BRRRRRRRRRRRRRT!!! Rupprecht proclaims, Mother of God! Billy Bob yells again, I'm warning you Paco, do not fart again! Paco clenches his buttocks but does not look like he can hold out for long. Now, what were you doing in that fermenter? Billy Bob presses. That fermenter was supposed to be filled with beer. Paco looks drunk and is soaked with beer that is beginning to smell stale. Rupprecht climbs the ladder and looks into the fermenter. It's empty and dirty, Billy Bob. Billy Bob yells at Paco, How the heck did that fermenter get empty? Where's all my beer? Paco belches and says, Uh... I drank it all? Rupprecht says, That's not humanly possible. Billy Bob is livid. What did you do, you little twerp? Did you have some kind of party in here? Did you think we wouldn't notice a whole tank of missing beer? Paco shrugs and finally loses his battle with his bowels, letting out another echoing fart. You're fired, kid! Billy Bob screams. Get out of my sight! I never want to see you again unless it's to pay for all that beer. Paco tells Billy Bob, still farting, I'm sorry, really. I'll pay for every penny of that beer. Billy Bob responds, Gull darn right, you will. Rupprecht escorts Paco down the stairs and toward the back door. Just out of curiosity, he says, why would you do such a thing? Paco explains, It was a lifelong dream to jump into a beer tank and drink it all. Rupprecht responds, Really? You poor, silly kid. Billy Bob calls from across the brewery, And just how do you plan on finding 20 thousand dollars? That's how much beer was lost. Paco tells Billy Bob, I'll work for free. Billy Bob responds, Not for me, you won't. You think I want to lose another batch of beer? Rupprecht tells Paco, You don't look so good, kid. You are swollen. Paco keeps farting and belching. Rupprecht yells, Get this man some Pepto Bismol! Billy Bob yells at Paco, No, get him out of here before I do something I'll regret.

4

Chapter 4.

Paco staggers slowly down to the river while talking to his dad on the phone. He explains how he really messed up and what happened. Also, that he's really sorry, but he owes Billy Bob twenty thousand dollars. Paco's father is truly flabbergasted. Wang asks Paco, Let me understand you correctly: You climbed into a fermentation tank and drank all Billy Bob's beer. Then you were caught red handed climbing out of the tank, drunk and soaked in beer. And in the course of one night, you managed to waste twenty thousand dollars of beer when you were supposed to be cleaning and preparing for a brew day? Paco responds, That's correct. I can't believe this. Look, I'll have to dip into my savings to pay him, but you go back and talk to him and tell him I'll personally pay him the money you owe him. Also, that if he'll have you, that you're going to work for free until you pay off your debt to both of us. You're going to be his indentured servant. Paco tells his father, Thank you dad, and I'm sorry.

Paco makes it home, and Hoppy looks at Paco and tells him, You look sick. Your face is swollen round, and did you pee yourself? Paco tells Hoppy, Yes, I can't stop peeing, belching, and farting. I may need to go to the hospital. Hoppy tells Paco, Drink water and take a hot bath. Close the doors and turn the shower on full strength with the hottest water. Take a jug of water and just keep drinking it. You'll be fine in an hour or so.

Paco tells Hoppy everything that happened. Hoppy tells Paco, People are going to think you're a real loser, but I don't Paco. You're my hero! You've got some brass balls and allowed me to live my dream. Somehow, I think Billy Bob likes you and will give you another shot. Paco says, Saavedra is going to break up with me, and my father is ashamed of me. Hoppy retorts, Everyone makes mistakes and deserves a second chance. Yeah, well, not everyone makes a twenty-thousand dollar mistake. Believe me Paco, Billy Bob has made mistakes too, and probably worse. Let him cool down, then go talk to him and be genuine. What about Saavedra? You're going to have to get going right now and talk to Billy Bob and hope for the best, because Saavedra wouldn't understand. Paco goes to take a shower and gets cleaned up then goes mimis. His plan is to go talk to Billy Bob after lunch when business slows down. Billy Bob needs time to cool off and will have time to talk.

Paco walks into the restaurant around 2 p.m. and looks for Billy Bob. Billy Bob sees Paco across the restaurant and turns red. He waves him away, but Paco shakes his head. Then Billy Bob points to a booth at the far end of the room, away from the customers. Billy Bob then walks over and has a seat with his Toque Chef Hat and apron. Paco immediately says he's sorry and that his father Wang is going to bring him the money. Paco also tells him that he'll work for free until his debt is paid. Billy Bob seems relieved to hear he can recover his money. He tells Paco, If you bring me the money that I've lost, then I'll bring you back as a brewer's assistant, but if you ever do something like that again, you better move to China or India or some place with a billion people so I can't find you. Paco declares his loyalty and gratitude and insists Billy Bob won't regret this. Billy Bob sits back and tells Paco, Heck, I've made quite a bit of crazy mistakes myself, but yours takes the cake.

Paco smiles sheepishly, then changes the subject: You know, I notice you have a slight southern like accent but you also speak Spanish. Yep, my father's side of the family is from the Deep South—Mississippi, Tennessee—and my mother's side is from Mexico City. I'm from right here in the borderlands, but people often think I'm not from here. Paco responds, I know the feeling. People don't know I speak Spanish and the Spanish I speak is from Southern Mexico. The foods and accents are different in the southern part of Mexico. If you go to the Yucatan, then it really gets different because it's unlike any other place in Mexico. Billy Bob adds, There are thirty two states in Mexico, all unique. Do you know what the full name of the country of Mexico is? It's not Mexico? Billy Bob corrects him: No, it's Los Estado Unidos de Mejico. Billy Bob goes on to say they should probably just change the name of the country to Mexico because nobody knows or uses the full name like here in the U.S.A. But the food from southern Mexico is truly amazing, he continues. They use more black beans, and even the tamales change dramatically in the Yucatan. I've even seen a tamale made of rice. There are several different variations as you go south. Paco responds, I love the infusion of different influences—the Asians contributed to the cuisine, too. My father told me Asians and present-day Mexico have been intertwined for hundreds of years. It contributes to having one of the greatest cuisines on earth. Billy Bob responds, I can talk all day long about food and drink. Get me some of your family recipes, kid, and we may just become friends after all.

Billy Bob goes on to say his Spanish and slang is Northern Mexican as with most if not all El Paso. Spanish isn't my first language. Paco responds, That makes sense, since you're kind of like a cowboy and Northern Mexico is Mexican cowboy-culture dominant. I've also noticed when you speak Spanish it has a slow drawl to it. My girlfriend, Saavedra, has Galician heritage. That's why her parents named her Saavedra, but she's really just an El Pasoan with Mexican heritage like me. My grandfather always told me that the Asian Mexicans are underrepresented in Mexico. Paco, hillbillies are a marginalized people, and guess what? The price of beef jerky is too high. I love having conversations with our youth, it makes me feel like people still care. My advice to you, Paco, is get involved in something. Go to town rallies, town hall meetings. Get to know your city and state representatives. That's if you want to make a difference. People like you could help change the laws, but nobody likes a back seat driver. In other words, don't complain if you're not making a difference yourself. If you are underrepresented, then get active and make a difference. Otherwise, you lack credibility in my view.

I've started to, but I'm really a passive person, Billy Bob. I avoid confrontations, and I get nervous. I just focus on beer. Billy Bob responds, Yeah, you have a moon face right now because you're still a little swollen from drinking all my beer last night. What's your deal, Paco? I've known you for a while now, and why are you such a mess up, always messing things up? Well, I've been thinking about that a lot today. I think that because I was severely bullied all my life that it's just affected me in certain ways. Billy Bob responds, How so? Well, in the 5th grade this bully flipped out on me and yelled at me from the top of his lungs and started to attack me. Then, I pissed my pants in front of everyone at recess time. Now any time somebody yells at me, I get startled and jump under a desk or piss myself sometimes. People always made fun of me, and not in a good way. In high school, this group of tough guys would follow me to class always raising their voices and making Chinese Kung Fu sounds right in my ear and in my face. One guy in each ear and the other in my face, everywhere I would go, all the way to class. It was so embarrassing. I was humiliated. I could never look people in the eye or interact too much with people, so I dropped out of school. My goodness, Paco, why didn't you tell somebody? It was too embarrassing, and I for sure didn't want my dad to know. My dad taught me Mexican Taekwondo passed down from generation to generation. The truth is, I probably could've beat up all those guys at the same time, but that's just it, nobody assaulted me. People just viewed me as some kind of reject. Billy Bob responds, You have to learn how to stick up for yourself because nobody else will. If you let people put you down or humiliate you, then they will. It's a dog-eat-dog world out there. I remember a conversation I had with you many years ago when you would come in the restaurant on your way home from school to grab a burger to go, and you told me you wanted to start your own brewery one day. Hypothetically, if what you said was true and you were going to actually follow through with your dreams, then believe me when I tell you, looking you square in the eye, that you will always be fighting and defending your business by any means necessary. It's just a part of life. You sink or swim, Paco, and it doesn't matter that you piss yourself, but you are going to have to fight in one fashion or the other. Normally, I'd tell you I don't respect a man that can't stick up for himself, but in your case it's not true. I'll make a man out of you yet, Paco. I've got to get going, I have to prepare for the Halloween Rock N' Roll Costume Ball this weekend. Before you go, tell your dad, it's okay. He doesn't' have to pay me the twenty thousand, but you do have to work your debt off. Paco says, Thank you so much, and I'll be here for the festivities with my friend Binky, he'll be dressed as a duck, and I'll be dressed as a dragon. Have I met your friend Binky? He doesn't sound familiar. What's Binky's last name? Paco thinks quick, but it's not his strong suit. It's Binky Jerkoff, he says. Billy Bob grunts. Huh, he must be Russian. See you and Binky later.

5

Chapter 5.

Paco walks home while calling his dad again and tells him the good news. His dad is relieved but gives him a huge lecture about being a Dong man and how his ancestors sacrificed for him to live a better life. I'm doing the only thing I know how to do, Paco, and that's being a Dong man. He goes on to tell Paco that his problems are self-inflicted and are first-world problems. Paco just listens to his father and is remorseful.

Paco walks in the front door and yells for Hoppy. Hoppy, I've got great news! Paco tells the duck-dragon all the details and Hoppy is happy for Paco. I have one minor detail that I left out Hoppy, I told Billy Bob that I was going to the Rock N' Roll Halloween Costume Ball with my friend Binky. Hoppy responds, who is Binky? You're Binky. I made up the name for you to be in disguise, incognito. You'll go with me being yourself, a duck-dragon, but you'll be Binky. One last thing, Billy Bob asked does he know you and what's your last name. I told him you last name was Jerkoff. Hoppy responds, You've got to be kidding me... my incognito name is Binky Jerkoff? That's correct Hoppy. You're my best friend, Hoppy, and Saavedra thinks the Sun Brewing Motel is haunted, so she wouldn't go.

Saturday arrives, the night of the Costume Ball. Hoppy calls for Paco, Are you ready buddy? Yeah, what do you think of my costume? You are a white aluminum can with four black capital letters B-E-E-R. You're a generic can of beer, Paco. Cute. Let's go, it's getting late.

Paco and Hoppy head to the brewery, meander their way to the bar, and take a beer menu from Chino. Chino's having a great time, cracking jokes and entertaining people. Paco orders a

Frankenstein Hybrid Ale and also orders a Canutillo Hoppy Vampires' Brew for Hoppy. Chino says, Coming right up. Chino serves the beers and says, Who's your friend? Him? That's Binky Jerkoff. Chino responds, That's one elaborate costume you have on Binky. You Russian?

Billy Bob comes out to deliver some food to some lovely ladies and they look at him and say, OMG! You have two different colored eyes! You don't say? Don't tease me; they're beautiful. We love you, Billy Bob. You all ain't had enough to drink to love me yet. Well, I love your country accent, Billy Bob. That so? And all this time I thought I had an El Paso accent. Enjoy your food, ladies, and bon appetit.

Billy Bob stops to talk to Chino. You know, Billy Bob, some people are still talking about how weirded out they are by your spontaneous fermentation tanks because of what happened to Isabella. Paco and Binky exchange looks. They know they're talking about a woman found dead in a fermenter not long ago. Billy Bob replies, I was running out of fermenters, and that one fermenter cost me over twenty thousand dollars. No way, I am retiring it. On a scientific level, we have powerful acidic sanitizers, but one could imagine how people would see the murder of Isabella sort of haunting our beers over all this time past.

Chino says, Aye… Billy Bob, the Rock N' Roll Halloween Costume Ball always makes me remember when me, you, and your wife ran this business back in the old days, just us three. You taught me how to brew, and we did it out of buckets. Billy Bob says, Good times, Chino. You, Chino, were my shelter from everyone. I'm not exactly a front-end guy. Good memories. You would have made a great Marine. You saved me many times from pouting over a bad review or from simply shoving a customer's face in my German beer chocolate cake. I guess personality goes a long ways. Time to get back to work, my friend.

Billy Bob has booked The Nobodys and Ray Arreola's band The Third Edge—two local bands that Paco knows he loves. They're starting to see people in interesting costumes such as Bob Ross or the most interesting costume of a Platano macho with two blue berries at the bottom. The Rock 'N' Roll Halloween Costume Ball was always a big party at the Sun Brewing Motel. Billy Bob, dressed as Frankenstein, starts the event off by playing classic Halloween music like "Monster Mash" and "Purple People Eater" by Bobby Pickett and The Crypt Kickers, then maybe a little "Thriller" by Michael Jackson, then he'll start to gradually increase the tone to "Don't Fear the Reaper" by Blue Oyster Cult, then finally to metal songs like Rob Zombie's "American Witch." He pairs Halloween music with Halloween beers and his Halloween cuisine such as Billy Bob's Frankenstein and Vampire cookies and Witches' Bread Fingers with Ghoulish Dip.

Paco says, Look Binky, there is some blonde running around dressed as Cinderella and is all smiles. Cinderella makes her way to the patio area and asks for Billy Bob to serve her. Maggie, the waitress, told her, He's cooking his Halloween concoctions, but he'll bring you some food if you order. Okay, then I'll order the Witches' Fingers with Ghoulish Dip. Can I also have a glass of The Monster's Bride? Paco orders the Werewolf Burger and Binky orders the Vampire Bat Ears in Frankenstein Barbecue sauce from Chino. Billy

Bob and Maggie deliver the food and Billy Bob tells them, Bon appetit.

Everywhere they look they see people in costumes roaming around the patio. The minister came as a Trooper Elvis and is performing real weddings over by the river. The last couple Trooper Elvis married had just gotten matching tattoos from across the street at Rivertrail Studios. Impulse tattoos, full motel rooms, flowing beer, yummy food, and getting married are commonplace for this extravaganza of an event at The Sun Brewing Motel.

Hoppy tells Paco, I don't know if you've noticed, but those two dudes over there not dressed in a costume seem to have been following us all night. Paco replies, Those are the same two guys who bumped into you earlier. Yep, and they've come a little too close for comfort a few times. Don't worry about them Hoppy. We're in disguise, and you're Binky Jerkoff. What made you choose the surname Jerkoff? I actually met one in Juarez. I met a few Russians in Juarez, and one of them had this high-pitched squeaky voice named Jerkoff. This may just work, Paco.

The local rock bands are playing, people are having a ball! The night winds down, people are about done and wandering about. They always wander to the back of the motel on the railroad tracks and to the river—especially the love birds who like to kissy-kiss in the dark under the weeping willow tree.

At closing time, people are still lingering and trying to sober up. The bands are done playing and Billy Bob as switched to a Spotify playlist. Another couple sneaks out to the willow tree at the back of the motel. Over the speakers we hear The Misfits' "Dig up them Bones." The couple starts making out by the tree, and soon enough it's starting to get a little heavy. They kind of swing around the tree, backing up a bit, but then they hit something hanging from the tree. We can hear the girl scream from the patio. Paco, Binky, and a few others run down there and see the blonde woman dressed as Cinderella hanging by her feet. The girl is weeping, now, and the guy is trying to comfort her while everyone gathers round and wonders what to do.

Eventually, the police show up. Jose "Pepe" Martinez III and his son Jose "Pepe" Martinez IV ride up on their horses. Pepe III is the local police detective and his son, Pepe IV, is the deputy. Both sport bushy mustaches, but Pepe III is more like a Hungarian handlebar mustache, something a real hipster cowboy would sport. Detective Pepe is a real-life inspector Clouseau in most ways except his eating habits. Pepe III loves to eat a lot of donuts daily. He's a bit large, short, and un-athletic, and it's hard to imagine him literally chasing down a criminal. Pepe IV is also short, but he's fit and muscular and reminds one of a rattlesnake.

All the witnesses are sitting on the patio not knowing what to say. The police secure the area, looking for evidence under huge floodlights. They try to record all the footprints, but probably several dozen people had been down there trampling about. They finished up taking their notes and people's statements and went away feeling perplexed.

Nobody had seen or heard anything unusual that night, and what kind of a lunatic goes through the trouble to hang a Cinderella upside down from a tree?

Paco and Hoppy start walking home down the river at night on the berm. Paco loves to walk down the river on the berm because of the way the moonlight cuts through the darkness and you can see everything happening on the river, but it's not always the same when looking up from the river. Sometimes you cannot see above so well, it depends on the placement of the full moon. Hoppy notices two guys walking behind them then speaks softly to Paco so as to not let on that they know they are being followed. Paco responds, Let's break off the berm and walk to that neighborhood over there and lose them.

6

Chapter 6.

Paco and Hoppy finally make it back home. They took a detour to make sure they lost the two guys from the Halloween Costume Ball that were following them. Paco sits on the sofa and Hoppy sits in the La-Z-Boy, both with their TV trays and Hungry Man TV Dinners. Hoppy has the channel clicker and puts on *The Mighty Ducks*. Fifteen minutes into the movie, they both pass out in their respective seats. Saavedra goes to Paco's house at sunrise, walks in the front door, and hears Paco snoring from outside. Hoppy wakes up with his fire breath and cries, Hi, Saavedra! Then Paco wakes up, a little disoriented, with blood-red eyes, then stands up and looks at Saavedra.

Saavedra tells them both, It's all over the news: There have been multiple murders at the Sun Brewing Motel. ABC local news is covering both murders—Isabella Mata from last year and Daisy Swallows from last night. I think you should find a job somewhere else, Paco, there is a possible serial killer on the loose over there. Paco responds, Aw, Saav, this is the closest I've ever been to my dream job. Plus I owe him a ton of money. Do it for me? she says. I'll see if he can make sure there are at least two of us on the overnight shift at all times, how's that? Well, okay.

Saavedra tells Paco, Let's go lay down in your room together. They got to his room and begin to cuddle on the bed, but Paco soon falls asleep and starts snoring again. So naturally, Saavedra turns on the tube to watch her favorite telenovela, *Tres Munecas*, with her headphones on. Paco is really tired and sleeps all day. Saavedra eventually has to get going to work and leaves a little disappointed after watching several episodes of *Tres Munecas*.

She's glad he's safe but a little put off again because she hasn't gotten much quality time with him of late.

Paco gets a very late start on the day and it's the early evening. Paco tells Hoppy, I'm heading out to the Sun Brewing Motel to go talk to Billy Bob. Hoppy responds, I'll go with, I need to stretch my legs and get a little water time. Nice, you make the swim beside me while I walk. Let's go.

Paco tells Hoppy, Wait for me in the water, and stay over there, kind of hidden in the shrubbery. I'm going to go try and talk to Billy Bob. Paco finds Billy Bob in the pub area talking to both Detective Pepes and walks right up to them to say, Are you talking about the Cinderella murder? Billy Bob responds, Not now, Paco. Come back tomorrow. Detective Pepe the Elder says, Hold on there, Paco. Did you see Cinderella last night? Paco says, Yeah, I seen her hanging from the tree with everyone else. The Pepes look at each other, and the Younger asks, How did we miss this guy? Who else was with you? Paco just looks at them; he hadn't counted on getting

Hoppy involved. Detective Pepe III gets impatient: Andale, Paco, it ain't multiple choice. Billy Bob answers for Paco, saying, He showed up at the Rock 'N' Roll Halloween Costume Ball with his friend Binky Jerkoff. The Pepes look at Billy Bob and say, You've got to be kidding me? Then they look at Paco and the Younger asks, You were with your friend whose name is Binky Jerkoff and you both witnessed Cinderella hanging from the tree last night? Paco mumbles, Yes. Paco, please go stand over there so I can talk with Billy Bob in private. Billy Bob, is that Paco Dong, Wang's son? Yes, it is. I see him walking down the river a lot. He lives in his father's apartment complex, right? Yes, he does. Do you know Binky Jerkoff? No, I only seen him in costume last night, but I think he's Russian and probably a great chess player and lover of vodka. I've been to Russia, there are certain things they all love. Alright, Billy Bob, we'll be in touch. The detectives walk away, while Pepe IV says under his breath, Hillbillies are always stereotyping people and butchering the English language. Pepe III responds, Billy Bob is supposed to be from here and even lived in Mexico. Pepe

IV replies, Hey dad, think about it. That would make him more Mexican than us. He's obviously not; he's kind of like a redneck, so it couldn't possibly be true.

Detective Pepe III tells his son, Keep an eye on Paco and do some undercover surveillance, because there is something off with Paco. He seemed nervous and evasive. I've also never heard of anyone around here named Binky Jerkoff. Billy Bob is right; he sounds Russian.

It's sunset, and Paco starts walking back to meet up with Hoppy in the river. It was a bad time to talk to Billy Bob, let's head back, Hop. Hoppy frolics in the Rio and swims close to Paco on their way back home. They get about halfway home and Hoppy flies over the shrubbery of the riverbank to walk beside Paco. They continue to walk half a mile when a group of guys come out of the riverbank off of a large, homemade pontoon boat/raft sort of thing made with plastic barrels.

They are all dressed in black ski masks, black sweatshirts, and black combat boots with dark blue cargo pants. They surround Paco and Hoppy and look very threatening. Paco tells them all,

With my right foot, I can kick your butts. With my left foot, I can kick your big mouths, and with my hands, one at a time, I can pimp slap your faces back and forth from the left to the right. Take a good look, you'll never see a Korean Mexican American like this again! I know Mexican Taekwondo! Then Paco jumps in the air and lands in a karate fighting stance while yelling, Heeee-yah!!

The men in black focus their attention on Paco and Hoppy. Hoppy doesn't say a word, but Paco says, You want some? How about you, peanut? You beanpole looking fool! Want some? Come get some. Then Paco starts making karate chop motions. One of them pulls out a dart gun and shoots Hoppy in the neck. Hoppy falls to the ground and passes out. Paco yells at them, What have you done! Hoppy has a freakin' dart in his neck! Then he runs at the guy who shot Hoppy and jumps in the air for a flying side kick, nearly knocking the guy to the ground. Paco starts fighting them all off and is taking major blows, Paco narrows in on the one who shot Hoppy and jumps in the air again, but this time lands a flying axe kick straight to his nose, then finishes with a front kick to the same spot. The guy collapses, blood spilling out of the middle of his face. While all this fighting was going on, Hoppy was taken on the raft with several others. By the time Paco notices, the kidnappers have already made it a good distance down the river. Both Detective Pepes catch the tail end of the fighting while trotting up on their horses. The men in black start retreating and disappearing fast.

Detective Pepe asks what happened. I don't know, Paco says. We were ambushed, and they shot Binky with a dart and kidnapped him. The detectives ask about the guy laying on the ground. I don't know. He shot Binky in the neck with a dart that looked like it could've pierced the skin of an elephant, so I kicked him in the nose a few times.

Detective Pepe Martinez III says, I'll call 911, and Paco adds, Maybe we should check his pulse. While Detective Pepe is on the phone, Paco pulls the ski mask the rest of the way off the guy's face and checks his neck for a pulse. Paco goes white and starts shouting. Somebody help us! Get an ambulance right now! I can't feel a pulse! Hurry!

7

Chapter 7.

The detectives take a statement from Paco and allow him to go home. As Paco is walking home, he feels a great deal of emotions. He is angry, sad, and trying to process it all. Paco gets home and immediately calls his dad and asks him to come over to talk. He tells him it's important but needs to speak to him in person, it's too important to talk over the phone about. His father shows up after a couple of hours with some tacos arabes. Wang tells his son, Let's sit at the table and eat these tacos arabes that I brought back from Juarez. Paco tells his father, those are some of my favorite, thank you dad. Paco grabs some tacos and Wang tells his son, We need to say grace to God for this meal. I know we should go to church more often, Paco, but please say a prayer to Jesus to give thanks. I want to be a better Catholic. I'm a religious man, too, Dad. Wang responds, Go ahead son. Say grace and pray to the Lord. Paco bows his head and folds his hands and speaks softly:

Bless us, O Lord, and these thy Arab tacos that we are about to eat. O Lord, thank you for opening your hand and giving us blessings. Please bless my beloved best friend Hoppy and look over him and protect him and bring him back home safe through Christ our Lord, Amen.

That was a good prayer son. Talk to me while we feast on these delicious Mexican tacos. I also brought several of your favorite salsas from my old colonia, Paco. Thanks, Dad. Did you bring me some Indio caguamons? No, Paco, I think you drink enough cerveza. You have a round face nowadays and are starting to get a little beer belly.

Now, what is it you wanted to talk to me about? Paco details all the events that happened since the Costume Ball. Wang is stunned and thoughtful. He leans forward and says, There is a famous Mexican detective named Egon Krahn with the Policía Federal Ministerial, also known as Mexican Interpol. He is also a private investigator. I still have a lot of old friends and connections in Mexico. I'll go track him down, talk to him, and set up a meeting between you two. I'm leaving now, I'll take my tacos to go. Keep the faith, Paco. I'm heading back to Mexico right now.

Saavedra is walking in as Wang is walking out. Wang smiles at Saavedra and tells her in passing, I brought tacos. You better get in there before Paco eats them all. Gracias, Señor Dong! Hi, Paco! Please sit with me, Saavedra, I have something to tell you. Saavedra says, I have something to tell you, too, but you first, Paco. Saavedra looks at Paco a little puzzled and tells him, For eating your favorite food and for cracking open a beer, you don't look happy, Paco. You look pre-occupied. Paco somberly fills her in. I told my Dad it was my friend Binky Jerkoff who was kidnapped. I didn't want to overwhelm him. You and I are still the only ones who know about Hoppy the Duck-Dragon. Paco, at some point, you're going to have to tell somebody about the duck-dragon. My father is going to get me in contact with a private investigator. I may have to explain it to him and hope for the best.

Paco, what I wanted to tell you was, Let's run away together. What? Are you crazy, Saav? Look around you, Paco. Murders are happening at the Sun Brewing Motel, and Hoppy was kidnapped. I care for Hoppy, but I love you. It's getting dangerous. I wanted to tell you that I was just accepted to a cultural exchange program from UTEP to travel to Madrid, Spain. It's for an entire year. Who knows, maybe we could build a life together in Europe? The Old World is rich in history, and most of all, not so violent. It's easy to go from country to country across the pond, Paco. It would be nothing to simply drive to Paris or Rome, and since you love beer so much, Ireland and Germany are right there, too. Paco tells her, I'm not saying no, but I need to find Hoppy first.

Of course, Paco. He'll show up soon. Hoppy is incredibly resourceful, and anyway, I'm not leaving for the cultural exchange program until after the springtime. Also, Paco, believe it or not, it's not just people from the Old World immigrating to the Americas. People from North, Central, and South America immigrate across the pond to Europe and other continents, too. Everyone is immigrating everywhere nowadays if they think they can get a better life. Okay, okay, says Paco. But I'm going crazy without Hoppy!

A few torturous days go by, and Wang returns with the famed Mexican detective Egon Krahn. I'll introduce you to my son Paco, then I'll leave you to do your business. You have everything you'll need, and if you need any more money, Egon, then let me know and I'll make the transfer. Wang opens the front door for Egon.

A short but serious-looking German-Mexican man steps into the front door of Paco's home. He has bleach-blonde hair with crystal blue eyes and is dressed very old-fashioned, with tan Wrangler rancher dress slacks and classic Mexican cowboy boots, a white button-up shirt, and a tan sport jacket. Paco, this is Egon Krahn of the Mexican Federal Police and a private investigator. He's here to help with the investigation into the kidnapping of Binky Jerkoff. Egon gets straight to the point. Paco, is his last name spelled J-e-r-k-o-v? No, it's spelled J-e-r-k-o-f-f. Hmm... that's interesting. Wang tells them he has to go and leaves. Let's sit at the kitchen table, Paco, and run through this forwards and back. Paco asks Detective Krahn, Where in Mexico are you from? Krahn says, I'm from Mazatlán, and my father and my father's father and their fathers are, too. Paco looks at Krahn's blond hair and blue eyes and thinks he protests a bit too much about his Mexican credentials, but he says, I've heard great things about the great city of Mazatlán. I've always wanted to take a vacation there and see all the unique culture from that state. Egon replies, Yes, and there's a great deal of German culture there. The Germans settled Mazatlán. All 32 Mexican states are different and known for different things, especially as you go south and on the coastal states. Your father told me his family is originally from Torreon. Yes, it's true, we're Asian

Mexicans. Paco asks Egon, Would you like a coffee or a beer or something? Egon replies, I'd love a coffee. Black, please.

Paco tells Egon, I have something to tell you that's going to be hard for you to believe. Only my girlfriend, Saavedra, knows. My dad doesn't know because I didn't want any issues and also because of the ancient folklore associated with dragons and ducks in our family. Egon looks a bit amused and responds, This should be good. Binky Jerkoff is a name I made up for my friend Hoppy. I actually met a Russian in Mexico with that name, so I used it for my friend Hoppy to go incognito to the Rock 'N' Roll Halloween Costume Ball at the Sun Brewing Motel. The thing is, I took Hoppy to the costume ball as himself. People thought it was an elaborate costume, but Hoppy is really a new species of what looks like a mix between a duck and a dragon. Egon looks at Paco, not sure how to take what he's hearing, and asks him, How did you run across this duck-dragon? I found an egg on the riverbank of the Rio Grande years ago, and I seen it hatch. I took the little duck-dragon home, and he became my family. I hid his existence from everyone because I didn't want no harm to him. I named him Hoppy, and he is extremely intelligent—on a genius level. He absorbs information like a sponge to water. He speaks multiple languages. Here... Paco pulls out his phone, searches for a video, and turns the screen toward Egon. It's a silly video of Hoppy playing *Grand Theft Auto*. He finds another video of Hoppy swimming in the Rio.

Egon still looks uncertain, but he's impressed by Paco's earnestness. He asks, Are you saying you think someone else knows about this duck-dragon character? Looking back, I think so, Paco says, because after the costume ball we were followed by two men. Followed? What happened? Me and Hoppy lost them by running through a neighborhood then circling back to go home.

Egon continues his questioning, taking notes and recording everything. Egon tells Paco, This is truly an amazing story, and I'll get to the bottom of it one way or the other. I should tell you I'm also well aware of the kidnapping of Binky Jerkoff from the local police force, and I'm involved in the investigation into what's going on at the Sun

Brewing Motel. Paco asks, Is there a serial killer on the loose? Is Hoppy in trouble? Egon replies, We don't exactly know yet, but a lot of people are looking into it.

Thank you, Paco, for your hospitality. I have a lot of people working for me undercover in the streets. We'll find him, Paco. Also, Paco, I don't think anyone has told you yet, but that guy that was unresponsive that you kicked in the face a few times, he died. We believe he is a Mexican national, which could create some problems for us and you, but it seems there is no record of him. Paco replies, Oh, god. I can't believe it. Am I under arrest? No, no, not yet. The Pepes saw enough to believe you're telling the truth. You may have to testify at some point, but you can say it was self-defense. It was! Yes, yes, I believe you. But how could there be no record of him? Egon tells him, In Mexico, people can just live. No ID, no record of birth, no nothing. He appears to be one of those types, but we have his finger prints and DNA now.

Paco is sad and going through a whirlwind of emotions but is staying hopeful. He tells Egon, Thank you, then shows him out.

8

Chapter 8.

A few weeks go by, and it's raining hard in November this year. Very few leads for Egon or the Pepes, but they push forward and are determined to resolve the many mysteries besetting them. Egon meets with Paco at his house to review the case.

Paco welcomes him into his home and offers him some coffee. Egon accepts with a smile as he slightly raises his cup to take a sip while nodding at Paco. Egon says, This is good coffee. Let's sit at the kitchen table, Paco. Paco asks Egon, Would you like a churro with your coffee? Egon replies,

Yes, I love to dip churros into my coffee. Thank you.

Paco, I've been looking at this from multiple angles. One of which is a missing person, but also, potentially, as wildlife trafficking. After all, there hasn't been any attempt to collect a ransom from you. Wildlife trafficking is a multi-billion-dollar industry and is a way for people living in poverty to make a lot of money. Juarez, Mexico, is a very large city with several million people in it. Juarez has a dark side to it, as does any other highly populated city, as you can imagine.

I've drawn circles and lines in red on this map of the tri-cities—Las Cruces, El Paso, and Juarez—from known wildlife trafficking cells or animals recovered. I also have a map of Mexico and the United States with more red circles and lines drawn. Nowadays, traffickers are also doing it digitally with social media, but they still rely on the underground networks. Technology is really aiding them and their networks; technology is a blessing and a curse Paco. It helps us find the bad guys, but it also helps them with organized crime.

Paco tells Egon, It's kind of a strange reality how technology can connect us around the world in an instant, yet it also seems to divide people extremely. Paco goes on to say, I think it's because the world is reduced to a meme. Egon replies, That's true. Honest discussions and nuance are thrown out the window without regard or empathy. Paco smiles and says, You're lucky you're old school, Egon. Why is that? It's because people like you don't get caught up in the mass hysteria and are comfortable in your own skin. Why, thank you, Paco, I still have my address book with everyone's number written down, and Egon don't text. Egon don't do social media neither. I like to have meaningful, face-to-face conversations. That's funny, Egon, I would've never guessed or pegged you for someone who would speak of himself in the third person. I was speaking to myself, but also to anyone listening, too. Paco smiles.

At any rate, Paco, I have my people investigating all leads. Eventually, something will show up, and we'll get a break in the case. Just stay patient, although I know it's very difficult. Thank you, Egon. Paco walks Egon out and shakes his hand with both hands to show his gratitude.

Holiday season is over and it's a new year. Still no Hoppy. Paco spent his holidays drinking and jobless while Saavedra is in her spring semester at UTEP. She's very excited about her cultural exchange program to Spain and feels happy. Paco has been down in the dumps and seems to have given up on life a little bit. He's always sleeping, which isn't like him, and he stays away from his dream job working in the beer industry at the Sun Brewing Motel. Paco also is starting to get messy and sloppy with his appearance.

Saavedra shows up at Paco's home dressed up beautifully in a yellow flowery sun dress with her long wavy dark brown hair. She had her French manicure and makeup job to perfection to accentuate her glowing hazel eyes. As she walks into Paco's home looking happy and beautiful, she sees Paco all sprawled out over the love seat, snoring loudly, with empty beer cans everywhere on the floor and end tables. She says, Paco, wake up! Paco wakes up with empty beer cans curled in his arms and as he stands up startled, the cans fall to the floor. Paco just stands there collecting his thoughts as he looks at Saavedra. Paco is all googly eyes for Saavedra and tells her, Saavedra, you are a sight for sore eyes. You look beautiful. Saavedra smiles and says, Thank you, Guapo. Let's get you cleaned up. Saavedra turns on the TV as she's picking up after Paco and sees a local breaking news story on KVIA-ABC news. Saavedra yells for Paco, Come here! You have to see this! Paco runs over and sees Saavedra watching the TV with shock in her face. She sees the Sun Brewing Motel on the news with legendary investigative reporters Iker Casillas and Elias Rockenstein. They're interviewing Peter François Amador, the Sun Brewing Motel manager, live on TV for a double murder where the bodies were found at their annual Keg Party on the Rio. Paco tells Saavedra, Look at all these web sleuths in custom Sun Brewing hats and T-shirts reading "Whodunit at The Sun Brewing Motel?" in the background. They are all milling about taking photos and video and recording themselves as if they're filming vacation videos.

You know what, Paco says, I should go down there. He runs right out the door before he can change his mind, and when he gets to the Motel the news crew and the web sleuths are still there. Egon Krahn pulls up just as Paco gets there. The web sleuths begin to gather round, sure he'll lead them to something interesting, while the KVIA team also grabs their gear and hustles over for an interview. Chino had been watching from the kitchen, and now Paco follows him as he runs to the brewery and says, Billy Bob, we got half of El Paso here. Maybe you should go talk to 'em. Billy Bob runs to the kitchen and looks out the window. Wowza, this is too much heat for me, amigo. Chino and Paco watch as he runs out the back door and around the patio and slips into his Volkswagen Beetle as quietly as he can, but when he starts it, everyone sees him and crowds around his car.

Egon Krahn had parked right next to Billy Bob's Beetle. He's there to meet with Texas Ranger Lt. Wienke and his trusty scribe, John John Coffee, along with both Detective Pepes. People are camped out holding different signs and shouting for justice. Sr. Egon walks up to Lt. Wienke and greets everyone. They're all collaborating in the investigations. Iker and Elias are still filming live for KVIA-ABC local news and asking the investigators numerous questions repeatedly, Do you have any leads on what people have dubbed the Poetry Killer? Do you think the Poetry Killer is responsible for this double homicide? Why does the killer choose the Sun Brewing Motel for his murders? As the news reporters are asking questions, you can hear people in the background chanting, Shut it down! Shut it down!

Saavedra calls Paco on his cell. This is one big circus and very dangerous, like I've always told you. Paco replies, They're calling him the Poetry Killer. Do you think it could be all connected to the disappearance of Hoppy? Saavedra replies, It has to be! Everything is connected to that brewery-motel.

Paco tries to get through to Egon, but the crowd is too thick, so he gives up and heads home again. He leaves a few messages for him, and Egon finally calls him back. Hi, Paco, sorry it took so long to call you back. It's been a hectic day here in Canutillo. Thanks for calling. Egon, is this Sun Brewing serial killer connected to the disappearance of Hoppy? As of right now, we see no connection, but I haven't ruled it out just yet. I'm keeping an open mind, but my intuition tells me they are not related because it doesn't fit the MO of serial killer. Most likely not related, but we need to solve these crimes and get answers. Thank you, Egon. Stay strong Paco. I'm working on it around the clock in full force.

9

Chapter 9.

Paco is spiraling downward and Saavedra feels it. Saavedra surprises Paco in the morning with his favorite Cuban coffee with cinnamon and cream and churros for dipping. Saavedra is all smiles and Paco's hair is sticking straight up and he is in desperate need of a shower. Paco looks at Saavedra, doesn't even tell her how beautiful she looks but does tell her thank you. Saavedra has the kind of beauty that wherever she walks, all men zoom in on her within a radius of eyesight. Wherever she goes, she pays no attention to others because she only has eyes for Paco and loves him. She sees things in him that others don't see. Saavedra is unique that way, not just with Paco but with other things in her life as well.

Saavedra says, Hey! Will you please accompany me to a birthday party my father's throwing for my mother? It'll be a lot of fun, Paco. My parent's favorite Galician family tapas and Mexican discada tacos. There'll be mariachis, which is your favorite, and most of all, beer too! It's an open bar, guapo.

I don't know, Saavedra. I don't fit in too well with your family. Us Dongs are simple people. Your family are highfalutin. It doesn't matter, Paco, just be yourself and be with me, please? I'll go with you Saavedra, no worries. Gracias, guapo. I'll pick you up this afternoon around four. Just be sure to dress nice for me, please. It's not formal, but look nice for me. Will do, Saavedra, and thanks again for the coffee and churros. You're welcome. Have a good day, and I'll see you this afternoon. Saveedra kisses Paco on the cheek and heads out.

Paco thinks to himself again about Hoppy. He thinks how Hoppy would be hyping him up, saying, Let's party, Paco! And how Hoppy always makes him laugh. They were true best friends. Underneath it all, Paco is losing faith but trying to keep it together.

Come afternoon, Paco starts to get ready to go to the party. Saavedra's father, Vigo Montelongo, is throwing a birthday party for his wife, Mela. Paco's thinking to himself, I guess I shouldn't wear my Converse All-Stars, but I'll wear them anyways with a nice pair of slacks and button-up shirt. Paco chooses his charcoal-colored slacks to pair with his Chuck Taylor All-Stars. These high tops are deep blue in color and in perfect condition—he takes good care of his favorite shoes. When Paco was younger, he would love to wear his flashy button-up dragon dress shirt, but this time he's going with a black V-Neck pocket T-Shirt.

Saavedra swings by again to pick him up, and when she unlocks the front door and walks in, the first thing she sees is Paco all cleaned up and looking sharp. She nearly shouts, Wow, Paco! Your hair is styled and you smell great! Must be the cologne I bought you. No, it's not Giorgio Armani Acqua, its Aramis. Oh wow, Paco, at least it's not Bruit. Bruit is actually my favorite, but I ran out a while ago. These have been collecting dust for years, and I know you love them. Well, what about me? How do I look? Beautiful! Now give me some sugar, baby. Paco grabs her and swings her down like they're ballroom dancing and kisses her. Now we can go, baby.

They walk hand in hand to Saavedra's Escalade, and Paco swings around to open the door for her. She smiles and then talks softly, almost whispering in his ear, are you feeling lucky tonight, Paco? Behave, Saavedra. Your father scares me. Saavedra kisses him and tells him, You're going to kiss me in my room tonight! Paco has the biggest toothy smile imaginable then runs around to the other side of the SUV and hops in.

They arrive at Saavedra's parents' mansion at the front entrance gate. Paco says, Please tell me the entry code isn't one-two-three-four anymore. Saavedra just smiles as she answers a phone call from her mom. Mila tells Saavedra, I'm so happy you're here a little early. Okay, Mom, we're driving in now, I'll see you in the house. The Montelongos' home is a huge mansion on top of the Franklin Mountains, built right into the slope. The road to the home is small and winding, going around the mountain and offering scenic views of the borderlands.

Saavedra and Paco drive up to the front door where her mother and the butler meet them. Mila is smiling as she goes to give Saavedra a hug and tells her, I'm so happy you're here, Saavedra! Then she glances at Paco and gives him an awkward smile. She grabs Saavedra's hand and pulls her to go into the house. Paco looks at the butler and says, What happened to the other guy? The butler replies, I don't know, sir. May I help you with your luggage? Paco replied, No, thank you. What's your name? My name is Ebert. I'll show you to your room so you may settle in for your stay. Please tell me I'm staying in the room next to Saavedra. No, sir. Mr. Montelongo gave me strict instructions that you are only to say in the yellow room. Which one is that, again? The yellow room is at the east end of the house next to Josue's room. Way over there? That's like the other end of the house from her. Indeed. I'll show you. Follow me, please.

Paco settles in his room then sits down and plays *Space Invaders* on his phone. Vigo Montelongo walks into his room and just stands there stoically looking at him. Vigo has a thin and very manicured English mustache and is always dressed up, at least in dress slacks. Paco looks up at Vigo and says, Buenas tardes, Vigo. Vigo slow smiles and says, Buenas tardes, I hope you enjoy your stay, then walks out.

Paco finishes his game then goes to look for Saavedra back downstairs and eventually finds her on the patio socializing with her friends near the bar by the swimming pool. As Paco walks up to them, he feels people are starring at him, but he ignores it and waves at Saavedra saying, A-ha, I've found you. Saavedra replies, I keep trying to go get you, but my mom keeps grabbing my arm and telling me, Don't go! Stay, please. Mila chimes in and tells Saavedra, Oh, come on Saavedra. Paco is a big boy and can find his way around. Plus, I want to spend time with my beautiful and talented daughter. Paco flatulates silently and pretends it wasn't him. He's degassing from drinking though his depression, having ingested an amazing amount of CO_2 over the last few days. It was silent but deadly. Saavedra, Mila, and a few others stop and look around and Paco simply smiles, then slowly frowns, saying, Who did this to us? Is there a sewage problem somewhere? Mila replies, There is no sewage problem here, and this horrid smell isn't from sewage. Saavedra just squinted her eyes at Paco. Mila grabs Saavedra by the hand and tells the ladies, Let's get away from here! I'll have Ebert spray the area.

Vigo and his friend Professor Plummer are talking to Saavedra's ex-boyfriend, Juan Carlos. Her parents invited him to the party because they've stayed friends with him and with his parents, too. They secretly always wanted her to date a well-to-do young man who is getting a top-notch education and whom everyone expects to become somebody important. Professor Plummer asks Juan Carlos, What are you studying at UTEP? I've just been accepted to medical school. Vigo says, Good man, Juan Carlos!

Paco meanders into the party and mingles the best he can, but he's always felt a little awkward in social situations, especially among the jet set that Saavedra's parents hang out with it. Professor Plummer, Vigo, and Juan Carlos have gone to the gazebo to smoke Cuban cigars and sip on some Pappy Van Winkle. Then they see Paco wandering about. Vigo calls and waves him over. Juan Carlos asks Paco, Mr. Dong, is it? Can I ask what kind of name is Dong? Where does your family come from? I've got Mongol in my blood, Paco says as if that were the kind of answer they were looking for. Professor Plummer frowns and asks, Are you sure it's not Chinese? I was always told I've got some Mongol in me, and my family comes from Korea. Juan Carlos laughs and says, So you're related to Genghis Khan? It's quite possible Juan, but I'm Mexican. Juan Carlos laughs again and replies, I'm Mexican. Why do you think you're Mexican, Mr. Dong? Well, for one thing, I was born there. I was born in Torreon, Mexico. Where were you born, Juan? El Paso, Texas. I'm going to tell you something else that's going to blow your mind, Juan Carlos. I don't speak your style of bro-

ken Spanish; I speak Spanish. I'm a first generation Mexican American, and I'm proud of where
my family came from and where I'm at now. I'm a
proud American. That's great, Mr. Dong. One last
thing that I've noticed about you, Juan, outside
of your cinnamon-red hair. You must have failed
social studies, history, and geography. Yeah, sure,
I'm in medical school. Aye, I hope you don't turn
out to be a surgeon because nobody would want
the wrong location to be operated on. Juan Carlos just smiles. You remember Professor Plummer,
don't you Paco? Yes, Saavedra's old tutor for many
years. Professor Plummer asks Paco, What are you
up to, nowadays? Actually, I think me and Saavedra are going to kick it in Spain for a while. Professor Plummer's face turns red and his eyebrows
scrunch together. Vigo bursts out, You can't be
serious. He then yells, Saavedra, where are you?
and storms off shouting, Come here. Now! Paco
watches him cross the yard and wonders if it
would help or hurt for him to get involved in
what's about to happen.

Vigo finds Saavedra with her mother and lays
into her, telling her angrily, I'm not sending you

to Spain for some romance with Paco! You understand me Saavedra! Paco has no ambition and will never be able to take care of you. Saavedra retorts, You don't know him, Papa! You've never given him a chance, never! He's actually a very, very smart man, Papa! I'll never forgive you if you get in our way. We love each other. Vigo takes a deep, indignant breath, his chest puffing out and his chin turned up, What did you say to me, Saavedra? Saavedra hunched over with her shoulders dropped with her hands up, tells her father, Please, Daddy, I love him. We'll discuss this later, Saavedra, but just remember this: You have your whole life ahead of you—and your education. Vigo takes one last look at his daughter then whirls around and storms off as angrily as he had come.

Saavedra's brother, Josue, runs up to the gazebo, grabs Paco's hand, and pulls him away. Josue cries, Let's get in the pool! Let's get in the pool, Mr. Dong! Wait, Josue, I don't have swimming trunks. Don't you worry, Mr. Dong, I already have some ready for you in your room. Let's go change. Josue, let go of my hand! I can go there just fine by myself. Josue just smiles slowly while lifting his shoulders a bit and at the same time slowly looks down. Let's go, Mr. Dong. Call me Paco, okay, Josue? Okay, Mr. Paco, but I love your last name.

Paco and Josue get to his room and Josue just looks at Paco with impish glee. Paco asks Josue, Can you go to your own room please? I'll be a little while; I need to shower. Okay, Paco, I'll be back. Paco was really buying time to take a couple of shots from a bottle of mescal he'd spotted in the booze cabinet, the kind with a scorpion at the bottom of the bottle. Paco cracks it open and takes a few shots to settle his nerves from this grand social event. Paco finally gets around to changing when he finally notices his swimming trunks are tight, underwear-looking Speedo swim trunks. He can't believe it, takes another shot of mescal, then puts them on. Josue walks right in and says, I'm ready! Let's go, Paco! Paco and Josue walk to the pool, both in Speedos, and everyone freezes and stares at them, some with their mouths open and others with their eyes wide open, too.

Vigo, Professor Plummer, and Juan Carlos finally notice Paco and Josue in the pool. Paco just jumped off the diving board doing a David lee Roth flying kick. Juan Carols says, Can you believe Paco is wearing underwear for swim trunks? They all just laugh. Evelyn the gardener walks by, and Vigo calls her over, Hey, Evelyn, come here, I want to ask you something. She says, Yes? Evelyn, if your boyfriend went to your parents' house for a party, would you be embarrassed if he wore Speedos? Evelyn answered, No, not at all Mr. Montelongo, but I would think it's funny, and the one thing Paco is, is funny. Paco is a different kind of funny. How so, Evelyn? Paco is funny without even trying; it just comes naturally, and I personally find men extremely attractive that are funny. I've always thought Saavedra is a lucky girl to have found Paco. There is no doubt Paco is funny and very handsome. Aye, I've heard enough. Thank you, Evelyn. Vigo then turns around and takes a few steps away from Evelyn while puffing on his cigar.

10

Chapter 10.

Mila's birthday party is still going strong into the night. The mariachis are done performing, but people are feeling the alcohol and still having a good time. Vigo gets on the microphone and says, May I have your attention, please. Thank you all for coming to my party for my beautiful Mila's birthday celebration. There are still tapas and alcohol, ladies and gentleman. My favorites are callos (chickapeas with tripe) and pulpo (octopus). Get some of them before I eat them all myself. Everybody please come to my table. This is a special, custom, black maple table—20 feet long. Please take a seat and gather around. As you can see, there is a line of Dom Perignon Champagne bottles. Grab a bottle everyone, we are going to make a toast.

Everyone is gathered around Vigo and the long table. Vigo looks at his son Josue and bids him to stand up straight. Josue snaps back, I'm sorry I'm not a macho man like Juan Carlos, Papa! Maybe if I was a macho man and going to medical school then would you love me, Dad? Josue, you're embarrassing me. Ladies and gentlemen, please excuse Josue, he's had too much tequila. Have I, Dad? I only drink sangria! Paco stands nearby, slightly hunched over, shoulders slightly dropped. He wants to tell Josue to can it, but someone else had taken control of his body. Josue looks at Paco, then he raises his fingers to his lips with a half-smile, puckers his lips and raises his eyebrows. Josue then looks around like his hand was caught in the cookie jar and runs off. Vigo then says, Josue is now cut off! No more booze for that guy.

Suddenly the cork in Paco's Champagne bottle pops off and Champagne gushes out everywhere. Vigo scolds Paco, You were supposed to wait for the toast! Paco looks around and says, I'm sorry, Vigo. It was on accident. Vigo's face is turning red and his veins in his neck are pulsating. Vigo says, Now then, everyone raise your glasses. To Mila, who is filled with beauty, riches, and love. She is worthy of it all, and may God continue to bless us. Salute!

Saavedra grabs Paco's hand and says, Lets go say our goodbyes then go to our rooms. I'm ready to call it a night. Me too. I've been ready for a long time, bonita. Just avoid my parents, Paco. Go straight to your room, and I'll meet you there to say goodnight. Paco walks into the mansion and sees Ebert and tells him goodnight. Ebert replies, Goodnight, and is Saavedra calling it a night too, Mr. Dong? Yes, Ebert, we're done for the night. It's been a great soiree. Paco continues to walk up the stairs and to his room. Josue comes in next and asks Ebert, Did Paco go to his room already? Yes, he did, Josue. He said he was done for the night. Saavedra comes in next and tells Ebert goodnight and walks to Paco's room.

Knock, knock, who's there? Saavedra just opens the door and comes in and hugs Paco. She coos to him, Thank you so much for accompanying me to my parents' party. Anything for you, bonita. Saavedra kisses Paco goodnight and tells him she'll wake him up in the morning for breakfast. Paco puts on his boxer briefs and white tank top undershirt then turns off the light and climbs in bed.

Just as Paco starts snoring, Josue sneaks into his room. He tippy-toes to Paco's bed and slowy climbs on top of the bed. He then puts his hand on Paco's shoulder. Paco snaps up, disoriented, and cries, What are you doing? Josue has had one too many drinks for the night and slobbers, Look, I brought Hostess Ding-Dongs. Paco is speechless, then Josue then bounces up and down on the bed softly while on his knees saying, lets play Ding-Dongs, let's play Ding-Dongs, let's play Ding-Dongs. Paco replies, play Ding-Dongs? Are you smoking bat kaka? No, Mr. Dong, I have a ding dong, and you have a ding dong. Let's play ding dongs! Paco jumps out of bed and says, Please leave, I'm trying to get some sleep. I'll have a Hostess Ding-Dong with you tomorrow with coffee. Josue replies, are you sure you don't want to play tonight? Please, Josue, please leave my room so I can get some sleep. Josue finally leaves, but now Paco is worked up. He puts on some shorts and goes looking for a glass of water.

He passes Professor Plummer coming up the stairs as he's walking down. He pauses at the foot of the stairs when he hears Mila speaking to the professor. You're wandering around late, she says. Do you need room service? No, I'm finally retiring for the night. Happy birthday, Mila. Then Mila says, Josue, what are you doing tip-toeing around the halls in your underwear? Get to your room. There is a patter of bare feet in the direction of Josue's room. There are heavy steps, and Vigo says softly, What is going on tonight? I've seen everybody sneaking around. It's kind of strange. Mila replies, Yes, it seems everyone's had one too many glasses of Champagne tonight. Vigo tells Mila, Let's get in bed, it's late. A door closes, the house is quiet, and Paco goes to the kitchen.

11

Chapter 11.

It's the next day after the soiree, early morning, and Paco wakes up to the sound of Vigo banging on Saavedra's door. He wanders out into the hall and comes up behind the man. Over and over, her father pounds the door. No answer. He keeps knocking more intensely while raising his voice, saying, Saavedra, please open the door. Professor Plummer comes out of his room to see what's going on, and the other guests poke their heads out, too. Ebert approaches Vigo. Would you like me to open the door, sir? I have the master key. Yes, yes, Ebert, please open the door.

Saavedra is lying in her bed unresponsive. He rushes to his daughter, tries to wake her, but she remains unresponsive. Call 911! Call 911! She is not waking up! Vigo screams. Mila runs into the room frantically screaming while hugging Saavedra, begging her to wake up.

Professor Plummer arrives at the door and scans the room. He turns to the others gathered in the hall and says, There's a syringe and a note. I'm calling 911. Everyone grows immediately agitated and begin talking about the Poetry Killer. It's his exact M.O.

Egon and both Detective Martinezes arrive at the mansion about twenty minutes behind the ambulance. Detective Pepe III asks everyone to gather in the living room while Egon and Pepe IV examine the bedroom. When they return, Egon scans the room and asks Vigo, Is this everyone? Vigo answers, Yes, everyone who stayed the night last night. Egon tells the detectives to make a list of everyone here right now and everyone who attended the party. The forensic team will be here soon, he tells everyone. We're treating this as a possible crime scene, so from here on out, no one goes into that bedroom.

Paco desperately wants to know what's going on, so he sneaks out of the living room and follows Egon outside and watches as he studies the estate. The mansion is awkwardly placed on the side of the mountain. The slope side is steep enough that no one ever goes there; it's far more pleasant in the front gardens. Egon walks down the mountain to the other side of the house, then squats down, pulls out a pen, and picks up a black leather glove with it. He drops it where he found it and immediately calls Pepe III. Is forensics here, yet? Well, when they are, tell them to get a team down to the south side of the house to gather evidence. Paco is studying the glove but can only conclude that it's very large, too big even for his hand. Egon snaps his finger at Paco and motions for him not to touch anything. Paco nods and backs away.

What are you doing, here, kid? Egon says. I had to know what's going on, Paco says. Well, just stay out of the way and don't touch anything, or so help me, you'll be next.

They continue down the mountain and reach the back of the house. Ego points to a door in the ground and opens it. Inside are old stone and cement stairs. Paco looks to Egon for reassurance, but Egon just grunts and starts down them. He has a small flashlight out and moves slowly so he can shine it all over. He stops and holds out a hand to stop Paco. He shines the light at a footprint on a stair. Stay here, he says, then backs up to the wall and sidles down the stairs. At the bottom, he finds an old solid-wood door made of oak. Paco can see him from the shoulders down. Egon tries to open the door, but it's locked. There's an arc in the dust here, he calls back. Someone has opened this door recently. He carefully backtracks up the stairs.

Egon sends Paco back to the house, where he finds both Detective Pepe Martinez III and Detective Pepe Martinez IV asking everyone questions in the living room. Detective Pepe III asks Evelyn, And who are you, ma'am? She responds, I'm the gardener. Now, as you may know, we're investigating the murder of Saavedra Montelongo. Evelyn says, But sir, how do you know she was murdered? Detective Pepe snaps back around and says, Who said it was a murder? Evelyn replies, Well, you just did detective. Me? And you are the geologist? No, detective, I'm the gardener. We will just see about that, ma'am. And who are you, sir? I'm Professor Plummer. So you're the plumber around here. No, detective, I'm a professor at UTEP. Okay, so where were you the night of Saavedra's murder, Professor? Here in the house like everyone else, Detective. Right. Doing what? I was sleeping, Detective. Suddenly they hear muted mariachi music blaring from Juan Carlos's pocket. Detective Pepe starts to do what appears to be a polka with a slight hop. Left foot, right foot, then a small hop followed by left foot, right foot. Juan Carlos says, Sorry, I thought I turned off my phone. Detective Pepe says, Dancing is in my blood. I do it naturally when I hear music. And who are you sir? I'm Juan Carlos. What are you doing here? I'm a friend of the family and was invited to party. Yes, of course, Well, please keep your phone off when I'm talking to you. And you, sir, why are you here? I'm Paco Dong, Saavedra's boyfriend. Yes, I know that, I know you're Paco Dong, Paco. Bad things keep happening around you, Paco.

The forensic team arrives and Egon takes them to several places in the house and around the house. He comes back with one of the forensic techs and asks who has access to the basement area in the far back behind the locked double doors? Vigo answers, Only me and the butler, Ebert. Egon replies, Ebert will you please remove your white gloves and give them to me. Ebert looks at Vigo, Vigo nods at Ebert and says, Please go ahead, Ebert. Thank you, Ebert. Now will you please get me a glass of water? Ebert replies, right away, sir, and marches out of the room. While he's gone, Egon shows the tech the gloves, making note of the tag and. Ebert comes back with the glass of water, and Egon tells him thank you and gives his gloves back.

Egon tells the Pepes that he's leaving now. Detective Pepe IV says, So soon? Don't you want to interrogate this group? Egon tells the detectives, I have what I need, but Vigo, please allow my forensic team to cover the entire basement please. They already have their instructions.

12

Chapter 12.

Both detective Martinezes finish up their questioning when they see Mila's face with tears falling and Vigo in agony and despair as he looks in physical pain. It's as if Vigo is walking around with a broken foot and trying to hide it. Detective Pepe tells Vigo, Thank you for your time. Vigo snaps at him, Get out! You fools! Vigo looks him dead in the eyes and sneers at the detective, I'm going to ensure you're finished in the borderlands. You are an imbecile! Detective Pepe replies, I always catch the bad guy. Detective Pepe then tells him, I'll escort myself out. Both detectives glance at Paco, one after the other, then leave the premises.

Iker Casillas and Elias Rockenstein arrive at the Montelongo estate filming live with ABC-KVIA local news. They catch both detectives Jose "Pepe" Martinez III and Jose "Pepe" Martinez IV leaving the mansion then swarm the detectives asking them question after question... Was this the work of The Poetry Killer? Has the Poetry Killer branched off from the Sun Brewing Motel? What happened here? We have information that there was a murder with a syringe in the Montelongo mansion. Can you speak to this? Do you have any information, detectives? Detective Jose Martinez III tells his son, I'll take care of these news reporters, mijo. Detective Pepe tells the news reporters, We have multiple leads already for this homicide, but we are not currently proceeding under the belief that there is any connection to the Sun Brewing case. Was she murdered, detective? Detective Pepe replies, There is some reason to believe so, Mr. Iker. He smiles for the cameras and turns away.

Paco wants a ride back to town with the Pepes, so he puts his head down and walks quickly off to the side of the house, hoping to skirt around the hubbub and get to the Pepes' car. The reporters see him, though, and everyone rushes over to question him. What's your name, sir? My name is Paco. Paco, thank you, what's your last name? Paco Dong is my name, and if you'll excuse me, I'm not in a good state of mind to talk about this. What happened last night? Can you give us any information? Paco replies, I'm sorry, I have to go. That's my ride.

The Pepes agree to take him back, and it's a long, windy, silent ride down the mountain. The Pepes drop him off at home, and he immediately collapses onto his bed and falls asleep.

Three days go by, and Paco is still in his bed. He hasn't watched TV or done anything; he's been near catatonic. He glances over at his phone ringing. He sees it's Detective Egon Krahn and still doesn't answer. The phone keeps ringing. The Egon calls back. Paco lets it go to voicemail. Finally, Paco picks it up on the third consecutive phone call. Egon tells him to meet him at the Montelongos' estate right now.

Paco gets Chino to take him back up the mountain. He arrives at the Montelongos' estate, and the butler escorts him to the living room. Egon has gathered everyone together from the party. Egon then says, Ebert, stay in here with us, please. Egon then makes a quick phone call. Now then, I've called everyone here to inform you we have found the killer. A team of police officers come in the living room as if on cue. The police surround Ebert and handcuff him. Everyone gasps with shock. Egon explains to everyone that he grabbed Eberts fingerprints off of the glass of water he gave him the morning of murder. He also tells them he had Ebert's glove examined with all the other evidence. Ebert is the brother of the man Paco killed in self-defense trying to save his friend Hoppy from being abducted. This murder was about revenge for his brother. They grew up as orphans in Juarez, Mexico, together. The murder was made to look like the Poetry Killer, but all the details were wrong, from the type and gauge of the syringe to the letter left behind. The fingerprints and DNA lifted where Ebert's and that's how we matched him to his brother. Take him away please.

Vigo, Mila, friends, and family, I am deeply sorry for your loss. Paco, come with me please. I know you're going through a lot, but let me give you a ride home. Paco takes Egon up on his offer and gets in Egon's car. Let me get you a coffee, Paco. You don't look so well, my friend. Egon goes through the drive through at Lucy's Café. How do you take it? Black, please. Egon smiles, then asks for two black coffees. I have something to show you, Paco. Do you mind going on a drive with me to White Sands? White Sands, Mew Mexico? Paco replied. Yes, there is only one White Sands Dunefield in the entire world. Why would we go there? I'll show you. It's not far from El Paso. It's maybe an hour drive or less. We're on the west side of town, so it takes the same amount of time to travel to White Sands as it does to drive across the city. Sure, let's do it, Egon.

Egon takes Paco to a secluded government building in White Sands that is fenced with a military-style entry checkpoint. They drive up to the checkpoint and show the military police their credentials and pass through. This is kind of scary, Egon. No worries, Paco, they are expecting us. This is like Area 51, Roswell type of stuff, Egon. Follow me, Paco.

Security buzzes Egon and Paco in the building. They are greeted by several government agencies for terrestrial sea, air, and land endangered species. There are even other government agencies for extra-terrestrial species visiting in the building. Paco and Egon are taken to a secure room with windows and a double mirror. When Egon and Paco enter the room...

Paco sees Hoppy – the duck-dragon!

They both run to each other and hug and kiss each other. They keep hugging, telling each other how much they missed each other. Paco's face has tears raining down it. Paco cries, You're alive! I was losing hope. Hoppy responds, They tried to sell me a few times on the black market, but the deals didn't work out so well. I think the kidnappers wanted more money than they were being offered. They had me in chains, but I'm a survivor, Paco. Paco looks at Egon and tells him, Thank you so much for finding him for me. It was a collaborative effort, and in a strange way, Saavedra led us to Hoppy. We broke the case open with Ebert's fingerprints and DNA.

Why is Hoppy here, Egon? The United States government is debriefing Hoppy on his rescue and trying to gain as much information as they can about him. It's not every day you meet new species, much less one that can answer your question. Don't worry: No harm will come to him, and he'll be home with you before too long. We'll stay for a little while, but we'll need to leave earlier than you would like. I've arranged for you to come by tomorrow for visitation. You'll be able to visit every day, Paco.

Paco asks Hoppy to tell him everything, and Hoppy gives him the major events, saying, "We can dig into the details later. I want to hear what's been going on with you." And so Paco has to give Hoppy the sad news about Saavedra's murder. They cry together over her death, and all too soon Egon comes back. Say your goodbyes, fellas, and let's go, Paco. I have something else to show you. They get in Egon's truck and take another drive. Paco asks, Another road trip, Egon? You'll see, Paco. I think you'll like where we are going.

Egon takes Paco to a famous mountain in the borderlands, Mount Cristo Rey. They walk through the desert and up the mountain. Atop Mount Cristo Rey sits a large monument statue of Jesus on the Cross; it's visible from the entire borderlands. It's on the border of Texas and New Mexico, and on the south side of the mountain is Mexico. Egon says, I'm very sorry for your loss, Paco. I know you've been through a lot. Know that Saavedra is looking down on you now, cheering you on. It's a long winding path up Mount Cristo Rey, and I make this trek sometimes because it's a form of cleansing for me. I think it'll help you too, Paco.

Egon and Paco continue their journey together and finally reach the top of Mount Cristo Rey. The wind is blowing hard at that high altitude, and they can see all of the borderlands from way up in the sky. They also see all the candles that were lit and crosses with pictures of loved ones by the colossal monument cross. I've brought a picture and a candle for Saavedra, Paco. We can light it together.

Paco says, Saavedra was my best friend and my everything. She was so beautiful and intelligent and most of all a great person. I never understood why she was with me. Every doctor, lawyer, and aristocrat wanted her. Egon replies, She loved you, Paco, and she will forever be in our hearts. Life can be tough, Egon. I don't know how I'm going to go on and find happiness, but Hoppy can help me though it all. This is like a nightmare that never ends, and I hope Hoppy recovers from all this too. Saavedra loved Hoppy like he was her brother.

Egon replies, Life simply isn't fair sometimes, but what helps us through it all is hope. Never give up, Paco. This just goes against the laws of the world, Egon. This life, this world, and this universe are too complicated for us mere mortals to comprehend, Paco. Have faith. Egon goes on, This walk up the mountain has helped you. I can see it already. Paco, I view it as Saavedra through her life saved another. I don't know, Egon, but I appreciate this hike up the mountain.

Here we are at the top of the mountain looking at one of the most beautiful monuments in the entire world. This colossal concrete white statue of the cross and Jesus. This beautiful mountain in the desert that has trees, shrubbery, and majestic vegetation in bloom. We are viewing the entire borderlands with the wind at our backs. We can see all the mountains and cities until the earth curves. This is divine and sacred.

Are you a religious man, Paco? I don't know any more, Egon.

Egon says, Being way up here looking over the borderlands is spiritual.

Have faith and hope.

Breathe the fresh air and be grateful for today.

The End.